The Turkey Who Came to Dinner

Based on the TV series *Rugrats*® created by Klasky/Csupo Inc. and Paul
Germain
as seen on Nickelodeon®

ISBN 0-590-66478-6

12 11 10 9 8 7 6 5 4 3 2 1   8 9/9 0 1 2 3/0

Printed in the U.S.A.   08

First Scholastic printing, October 1998

The Turkey Who Came to Dinner

Adapted by Kitty Richards
from the Script by Mark Palmer
Based on the Story by Laine Raichert, J. David Stem, and David N. Weiss

Illustrated by Ed Resto

SCHOLASTIC INC.
New York Toronto London Auckland Sydney

It was Thanksgiving Day. At the Pickleses' home, everyone was busy. Didi was telling Tommy, Phil, and Lil about the celebration of Thanksgiving. Stu and Drew were setting up lots of TVs and satellite dishes so they could watch every football game in the country.

Angelica was watching the Macy's Thanksgiving Day Parade on TV while Grandpa Boris snored on the couch. Everyone else was in the kitchen, arguing about what to make for dinner.

Dingdong! Didi answered the door. It was Chuckie and his dad.

"Why do you guys gots feathers on your heads?" Chuckie asked the other Rugrats.

"We're playing Nakie Americans," said Tommy. He put a feathered headdress on Chuckie.

"Do I gotta take my clothes off?" Chuckie asked nervously.

"No, Chuckie," said Tommy. "It's Hanks Giving!"

"Who's Hanks Giving?" Chuckie wanted to know.

"It's not a person, Chuckie," Tommy explained. "It's the day we have a big dinner with our fambly and friends and 'member how happy we are."

So the Rugrats sat down for a tasty, make-believe Thanksgiving dinner of Reptar cereal—and also some crackers they found under the couch.

In the meantime everyone was waiting for Grandpa Lou to bring home the Thanksgiving turkey. He soon came back with a bag. He reached in and pulled out—a trophy!

"Pop!" cried Didi. "You did buy our turkey, didn't you?"

"I did better than that," said Grandpa Lou. "I *won* a turkey. They said it'd be here by four at the latest."

Four o'clock! That was way too late! Didi, Minka, Charlotte, Betty, and Howard hopped in the car and raced to the grocery store. They needed a turkey right away.

Just then there was a knock at the door. It was a delivery man carrying a big box. He woke Grandpa Boris.

"What? Can't you see I'm sleeping?" asked Boris.

"Look, I'm sorry to bother you," said the delivery man. "But I've got a turkey here. Where should I put it?"

Boris sighed. "Where else does a turkey go on Thanksgiving?" he said. "In the kitchen!"

"Thanks," said the delivery man. Boris fell back to sleep.

 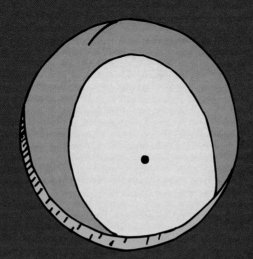 

The Rugrats followed the delivery man into the kitchen. He placed the box on the floor and left. The babies stared at the box. What could be inside? Chuckie screwed up his courage and took a peek. A pair of beady black eyes looked back at him.

"There's something in that box," Chuckie whispered as he quickly backed away.

Tommy toddled over and knocked on the box. "Hello?" he said.

The box began to shake. Suddenly a flapping, gobbling creature burst out!
"Aaaaaaahhhhhhh!" the Rugrats screamed.

It was a real, live turkey!

Tommy wanted to invite it to dinner. But Chuckie wasn't sure. "He's awful scary looking," he said.

Chuckie may not have liked the turkey, but the turkey sure liked Spike!
Everywhere Spike went, the turkey trailed behind him. It followed the dog all
around the yard, and the Rugrats were right on its tail.

Just then Angelica appeared. "What are you doing with that turkey?" she asked.

"We're trying to ask him to come to our dinner," said Tommy.

"Oh, he's comin' to dinner, all right," said Angelica. "He's gonna *be* dinner!"

The Rugrats gasped. You were supposed to say thank you to your friends on Thanksgiving—not eat them!

"We've got to get him out of the yard!" said Tommy. "I think he's a bird. Maybe he can fly."

Meanwhile Grandpa Boris finally woke up. Grandpa Lou had found the empty box and wanted to know where his turkey was.

"A delivery man came a little while ago," explained Boris. "I told him to put your turkey in the kitchen."

"Well, he's not here now," Lou said as he put on a helmet. "It must be in this house somewhere."

He grabbed a big net and then he grabbed Boris. The two men started their search.

In the backyard the Rugrats were flapping their arms, hoping the turkey would get the picture. It didn't.

They tied a string around the turkey's neck and tried to make it run fast so they could fly it like a kite. That didn't work either.

Finally, the babies put the bird on one end of the teeter-totter and jumped on the other end. But it was no use. The turkey would not fly away.

Just then Didi and the gang returned from the grocery store—with no turkey. They did have a frozen turkey dinner, turkey franks, and turkey pastrami. Everyone was still arguing, and they all raced to the kitchen to use the microwave.

Meanwhile Lou and Boris spotted the turkey in the backyard.
They chased it with their net as the poor bird ran around in circles.
Angelica joined in too.

Suddenly Angelica tripped. Boris and Lou jumped over her and landed on one end of the teeter-totter. At the same time, the turkey landed on the other end.

"Gobble! Gobble! Gobble!" squawked the frightened turkey as it flew through the air, flapping its wings.

It looked like the turkey was going to make it, when it flew right into the tower of satellite dishes. *CRASH!* The dishes toppled to the ground. So did the turkey.

In the living room every TV set had been tuned to one very exciting football game. Stu and Drew were on the edge of their seats.

Suddenly all the TVs fizzled out.

In the kitchen the microwave—with all the food inside—exploded!

"Oh, no!" cried Didi. "The kids!" Everyone ran outside.

There was no need to worry. The Rugrats were fine. But what about the turkey? Everyone held their breath.

Finally, under the pile of satellite dishes, something moved. The turkey popped his head out. The Rugrats smiled—their new friend was okay!

"That thing ruined our football game!" shouted Stu.

"It ruined our dinner!" added Betty. Everyone murmured in agreement.

"Well, dinner's not quite ruined," said Drew. "We've still got turkey."

All the grown-ups took a step toward the frightened bird.

The Rugrats held hands and formed a line to protect the turkey.

"What are the kids doing?" someone asked.

"Maybe they think we want to eat it," Chaz said.

"Well, don't we? It ruined our Thanksgiving," said Betty.

Finally Didi spoke up. "No," she said. "This turkey didn't ruin our Thanksgiving. We did. We spent the whole day arguing about what to eat and what to watch.

Thanksgiving isn't about football, or food, or parades. Thanksgiving is about family and friends."

Everyone looked around sheepishly. They knew Didi was right.

Boris broke the silence. "Friends I like, but what are we going to eat? Everything is kaput!" he said.

So Tommy shared his Thanksgiving dinner. Everyone feasted on Reptar cereal and milk. Spike even shared his food with the turkey.
It was a "Hank's Giving" no one would soon forget!

THE FIRST THANKSGIVING

In 1620 a group of people left England because the king would not let them pray in their own way. They sailed on a ship called the Mayflower for sixty-six long days over rough seas. They finally landed at Plymouth Rock, in what would later be called Massachusetts.

Life was not easy for the people we now call the Pilgrims. Their first winter was very hard. Nearly half of the Pilgrims died.

But that summer their Native American friend, Squanto, showed them where to hunt and fish, and how to grow food like corn and pumpkins. That fall the Pilgrims had a good harvest. It was time for a celebration! They invited their new friends and had a three-day feast. They ate turkey, goose, venison, eel, corn, dried plums, berries, beans, and lots of other things.

Now we too give thanks on the fourth Thursday of each November. We remember the Pilgrims of long ago. We eat food like turkey and stuffing and cranberry sauce. But we *don't* eat eels!